Published and distributed by

ISLAND HERITAGE
P U B L I S H I N G

94-411 KŌ'AKI STREET, WAIPAHU, HAWAI'I 96797-2806
Orders: (800) 468-2800 • Information: (800) 564-8800
Fax: (808) 564-8877 • www.islandheritage.com

ISBN# : 0-89610-347-1

First Edition, Twenty-second Printing - 2011
COP101312

HUMU

The Little Fish
Who Wished Away His Colors

Written by
Kimberly A. Jackson

Illustrated by
Yuko Green

DEDICATION

To the colors in my life, Greg and Keli – *Kimberly Jackson*

For Bob & Hazel – *Yuko*

In the ocean waters surrounding a lovely island lived a beautiful fish who had many colors. He was turquoise blue above his eyes, along his back, and on the tip of his snout. On his sides were red marks and yellow lines. He was truly a wonder!

He was also very shy.

The little fish lived in Hawaiian waters. His Hawaiian name was humuhumunukunukuāpua'a. His name was really hard to say, so his friends just called him Humu.

Humu wished he wasn't such a colorful fish. Humu wished he could blend into the background like a moray eel hiding in a crevice, for Humu was very shy.

One of Humu's friends was all yellow. She had no other colors on her body.

Her Hawaiian name was lauʻīpala, but her friends called her Tang.

Another of Humu's friends was all red.

His Hawaiian name was ʻāweoweo, but his friends called him Red

4

Many of the other fish in Humu's waters had a lot of colors and patterns. But Humu didn't notice the other fish. All he noticed was that his best friends were all one color.

Humu thought he looked silly. He wished he could be all one color just like Tang and Red.

Humu decided to drape seaweed on his back and around his tail to hide all his colors. When Humu put the seaweed on, he did look silly!

His friends laughed.

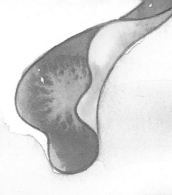

Humu did not understand that they were laughing at how silly he looked in the seaweed. He began to think that his friends didn't like him.

Humu decided to swim away.
He decided to swim far, far away.

Humu swam for a long time.

He decided to rest on the ocean floor, but he didn't see a sea urchin at the spot where he touched. "Ouch!" said Humu

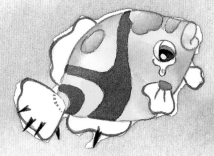

Humu swam away even faster.

He swam

and

he swam.

Humu was starting to get scared. He had swum far, far away from his home. Humu had never been so far before. He looked ahead and saw a big sea turtle swimming along. "Honu," called Humu, thinking the turtle was his friend from home. But this sea turtle did not know Humu and swam on.

Humu saw a manta ray and he tried to swim fast enough to catch up with it, but the manta ray was too fast. Humu couldn't reach her.

Humu was now very far from home. He dove to the bottom of the ocean and started to cry.

A large humpback whale named Misty heard Humu crying. Misty was a special whale because she could do magical things. She swam over to Humu. "Little friend," Misty whispered, "what is wrong?"

Humu had heard of humpback whales, but he had never seen one of the huge creatures before. Misty was very big. Humu started to quiver.

"Do not be afraid, little fish," Misty said gently. "I want to help you. What is wrong?"

"I don't like my colors!" quaked Humu. "I wish I was all one color. I wish I could blend right in with the sand." Humu thought a bit more and then blurted, "Yes, I wish I WAS the color of sand. Then I could blend into the ocean bottom."

"Are you sure you want to be the color of sand?" asked Misty.

"Yes," cried Humu, "I am sure!"

"Well," said Misty, "I am a magical whale and I can grant one wish to you. I can change you to be the color of sand."

"Oh, please, please do," moaned Humu.

13

"Okay," said Misty, "but if in three days you decide you want your old colors again, come right back here and call my name. I will give you back your colors. If you don't come in three days, you will be sandy-colored forever."

"Alright," said Humu, barely hearing the part about three days. "All I want is to be the color of sand. Please hurry so that I can swim back to my home. Hurry!"

15

With a wave of her tail and a twitch of her flippers, the whale started to slowly spin. Then she blew out some magic bubbles through the top of her head and the bubbles surrounded Humu.

And,

with a

swoosh...

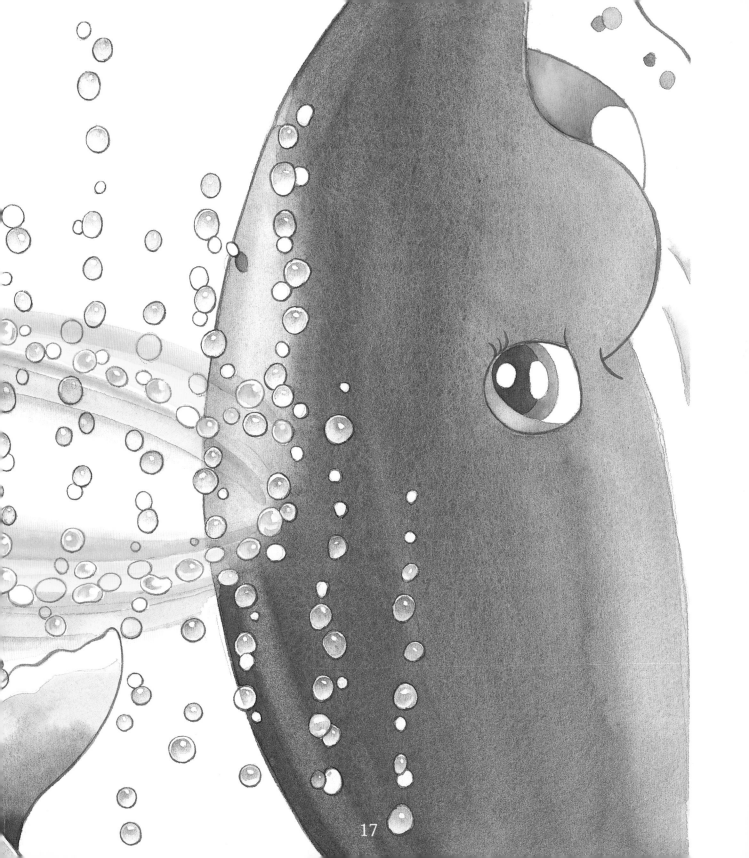

Humu was the color of sand.

"Oh, thank you, thank you,"
said Humu, "now I must return to my home."

"But remember, you can get back your colors if you return in three days," Misty reminded him, for she was wise and knew Humu was making a mistake.

"Oh, I will," said Humu, although he couldn't imagine he'd ever again want the turquoise blue, red, and yellow colors.

"Aloha,"
Humu said as he swam home as fast as he could.

19

Humu's friends
were very worried.
They had not seen
him for more than a day.

Just then, Humu swam
right up to his friends
and rested near them.

"Tang, Red," Humu called,
"I'm back!"

But Tang and Red could not see him. They looked all around.

"Where are you?" they both chimed. "We hear you but
we can't see you!"

"I'm at the bottom," Humu answered.
Tang and Red looked down and could
not believe their eyes.

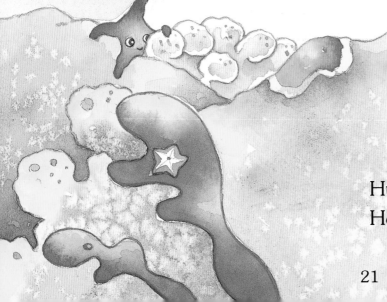

Humu's beautiful colors were gone.
He was the color of sand!

"What happened to your colors?" cried Red and Tang.

"If someone took your colors, we'll go get them back. We want to talk to whomever did this."

Humu was puzzled. He thought his friends believed he looked silly with all his colors. Humu told Tang and Red how Misty had granted his wish to be the color of sand.

"Oh, Humu," Tang said sadly. "I should have told you how beautiful you are— I mean were. Then this would never have happened."

"Me too," said Red. "I should have told you how nice you look, I mean looked."

"Humu, we like you however you are," said Tang. "You are very beautiful as a sandy-colored fish or as a fish with many colors."

"Yes," agreed Red. "We like you just how you are."

Just then Humu remembered that Misty had promised he could get back his colors. But, he had to return to the whale spot within three days and call for Misty!

How many days had it been since he left the whale? It had been a long swim home. It had taken him more than a day. He knew that he must reach the whale in half a day or he would be sandy-colored forever.

Humu quickly explained to his friends, "If I hurry, I can make it back to the spot. I must go now!"

"We'll help you!" answered Red and Tang. "You lead the way!"

Humu and his friends swam as fast as they could.

At last they reached the spot where Humu had met Misty.

"MISTY, MISTY!" yelled Humu. "YOU WERE RIGHT. PLEASE GIVE ME BACK MY COLORS."

"PLEASE MAKE ME THE WAY I WAS BEFORE. PLEASE, MISTY, PLEASE!" begged Humu.

But Misty did not answer. The only sounds were the echoes of Humu's words off the surrounding coral reef. Tang and Red looked sadly at each other.

"Oh, maybe I'm too late," cried Humu. "Maybe I'll stay the color of sand forever because I was too silly to like myself just the way I was. PLEASE, MISTY. I MADE A MISTAKE."

All of a sudden a bubble started to form far above Humu. The bubble swirled round and round and changed to a stream of bubbles. The stream then formed a rainbow of colors and was like a JACKET for Humu. The jacket had exactly the same colors and patterns that Humu had before he made his wish.

"Humu, look up!" Tang yelled. "Look what is coming toward you." The jacket was now shimmering and gently floating toward the bottom. Misty had kept Humu's colors somewhere and was now giving them back!

Humu looked up, then darted up and swam right through the quivering shape.

ZIP zip, the jacket fastened on Humu and became part of him again.

Humu had his old colors back. He was overjoyed!

The fish cheered. Once again Humu was himself.

"Let's go home," said Humu. Then he stopped briefly and glanced back to the magic spot.

"Thank you, Misty," Humu whispered. "Thank you for being so wise."

Humu and his friends swam off happily to home waters.

THE END